To Linda and Walter —E. P.

To Victor —C. S.

Library of Congress Cataloging-in-Publication Data

Pilgrim, Elza.

The china doll / Elza Pilgrim; illustrated by Carmen Segovia.

p.   cm.

Summary: A china doll sets out on a perilous adventure
in search of the perfect birthday present for her owner.

Sterling ISBN 1-4027-2223-0

[1. China dolls—Fiction. 2. Dolls—Fiction. 3. Adventure and adventurers—Fiction.
4. Gifts—Fiction. 5. Birthdays—Fiction.] I. Segovia, Carmen, ill. II. Title.

PZ7.P6293Ch 2005   [E]—dc22   2005008797

10   9   8   7   6   5   4   3   2   1

Published by Sterling Publishing Co., Inc.

387 Park Avenue South, New York, NY 10016

Text copyright © 2005 by Elza Pilgrim

Illustrations copyright © 2005 by Carmen Segovia

Distributed in Canada by Sterling Publishing

c/o Canadian Manda Group, 165 Dufferin Street,

Toronto, Ontario, Canada M6K 3H6

Distributed in Great Britain and Europe by Chris Lloyd at

Orca Book Services, Stanley House, Fleets Lane, Poole BH15 3AJ, England

Distributed in Australia by Capricorn Link (Australia) Pty. Ltd.

P.O. Box 704, Windsor, NSW 2756, Australia

Sterling ISBN 1-4027-2223-0

For information about custom editions, special sales, premium and
corporate purchases, please contact Sterling Special Sales
Department at 800-805-5489 or specialsales@sterlingpub.com.

The China Doll

Elza Pilgrim

Illustrated by

Carmen Segovia

Sterling Publishing Co., Inc.
New York

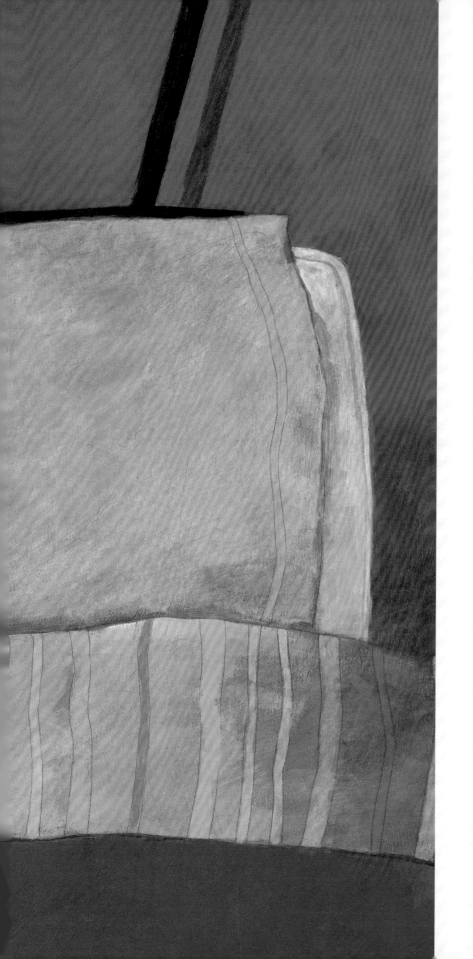

The china doll turned her black eyes up to the face of the girl who was hugging her so tightly in her sleep. The child, Jessica, was good and fair, and she had always been kind to her toys—especially Sarah, her china doll. Sarah was only too happy to belong to the girl.

Sarah had been waiting for Jessica's fifth birthday for what seemed like forever. She knew exactly what she wanted to get her, too: a tea set. It was the perfect gift. A pretty little tea set would allow them to share a cup of tea during playtime. There was only one problem. Where was a china doll going to find such a gift?

The doll carefully wiggled herself from the arms of her owner and moved to the end of the bed. From there she climbed down to the floor. She stood silently for a few moments, at a loss for what to do. Where should she start?

A fly flew by her face. "One moment, Mister Fly, if you please," the china doll called out. "Can you tell me where I can find a tea set?"

"Hey, Buzzzter! That's Mizzz, not Mizzzter!" replied the fly indignantly.

The china doll blushed at her mistake. "Please forgive me," she said. "Still, would you happen to know where I can find a tea set?"

"Ask the ratzzz," buzzed the fly. "They know where everything izzz. Now buzzzz off!" It flew away up to the lamp.

"Thank you," said the china doll politely. The fly hadn't exactly been friendly, but at least it had been helpful. Now all she needed to do was find those rats the fly had mentioned.

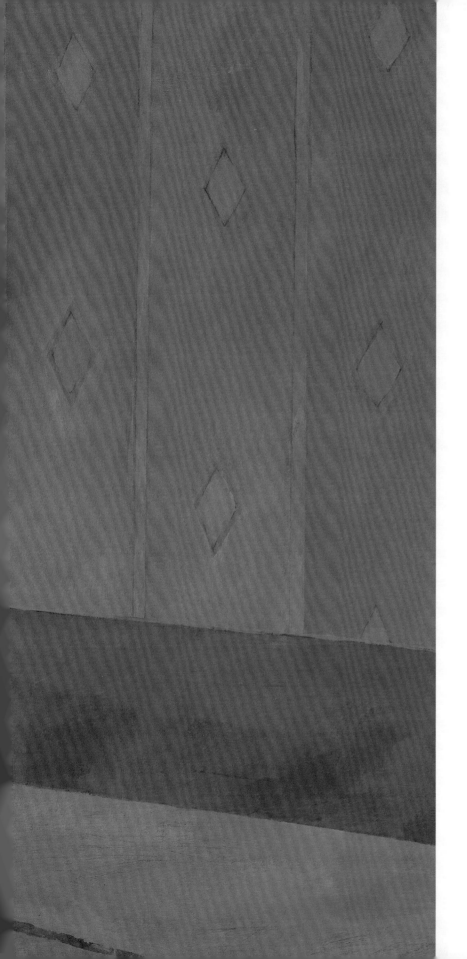

On one wall of the bedroom was a small crack. As the doll glanced at it, she thought she saw a flicker of movement. All at once, she was frightened. What if rats were terribly unpleasant? Before she had time to think about it, she heard a voice by her ear.

"What do you want?" the mysterious voice whispered.

"Are you . . . a rat?" Sarah breathed softly.

"I am," the creature answered. "Who are you, and why do you want to know?"

Sarah took a deep breath. "I was told you would be able to help me," the china doll began. "I need to know . . . "

"It will cost you," the rat whispered.

"I haven't even asked you yet," protested the china doll. "What if you can't help me?"

The rat smiled. "I know everything."

"What do you want in exchange?" Sarah asked anxiously.

The rat sniffed about. "I like your hat," it finally whispered. "An answer for a hat."

$\mathcal{S}$arah touched the lace bonnet atop her silky black curls. The thought of Jessica waking up to a beautiful tea set gave the china doll the courage to untie the bonnet and hand it to the rat.

"Ah, now," said the rat. "What would you like to know?"

The china doll spoke softly. "I would like to know where I can find a tea set."

The rat thought for a moment. "There is something," it said. "Yes, I can help you. You will need a key. Wait here and I will fetch it for you." The rat scurried off and was gone for quite some time. The china doll wondered if it had forgotten about her—or had decided not to come back after all. Finally she heard the sound of tiny paws approaching. In the rat's mouth was a large brass key with a red ribbon, which it dropped on the floor in front of Sarah. "The key unlocks a treasure chest," the rat told her. "The chest is in a big barn and it is filled with all sorts of magnificent things. You will find a tea set there."

"Thank you! Oh, thank you!" exclaimed the little china doll. She took the key. It was almost half as tall as she was.

"Follow me," directed the rat. "I can take you as far as the end of the house."

The rat led Sarah through dark tunnels and cracks. "Here we are," it announced finally, standing outside on some grass.

The china doll held her breath. The outside world was so big and dark it seemed to swallow her up. She heard sounds she had never heard before. But there ahead of her was the barn the rat had told her about. Somewhere inside it was the treasure chest. For that treasure chest, Sarah could be brave.

Suddenly a loud squeal made Sarah spin around. A large animal was about to pounce.

"Food!" cried a leaping cat with gleaming eyes.

"Fiend!" cried the rat, narrowly escaping the cat's claws. In a flash it retreated back into the tunnels, leaving Sarah to fend for herself.

The cat circled the china doll, eyeing her curiously. "What have we herrre?" it purred.

"The cat can't eat me," Sarah thought to herself, trying to stay calm. "I'm made of china and cloth. But it's still such a frightening creature."

As if it had heard her, the cat continued, "You look like a cherrrished playmate. I've always wanted a friend, and neowwww I have one!" The cat grinned. "I think I shall toss my new plaything up in the air!" With a flick of its paw, the cat sent the china doll flying.

Sarah hit the ground with a bounce. The cat scampered over to toss her again.

"Please, no more!" begged Sarah. "That is not how you play with a doll. I am very delicate and this kind of play will break me!"

The cat looked as if it had no intention of stopping, but suddenly a barking sound interrupted them. The cat streaked across the yard as fast as it could go and wriggled under the fence just as a much bigger animal ran around the corner. It barely missed stepping on Sarah with its big furry feet.

"Rrff! Get back here!" the large dog growled, chasing after the cat.

The two animals disappeared beyond the fence and the china doll was left alone. She sat up in the grass and looked down at herself. What a mess she was! No bonnet to keep her hair neat and grass stains all over her dress. Sarah wiped some dirt from her face with her silk apron. As she did, she felt a narrow crack along her forehead, down to her eyebrow.

"Oh, no!" cried the china doll. "I am broken! Who will want to play with a broken doll?" She stood up and looked at the barn. Was it worth it? If she had only stayed in bed with Jessica, she would still be good as new. Then she closed her eyes and pictured sitting down to a lovely tea party with Jessica, having a grand old time. She started toward the barn.

Inside the barn was new and strange. There were many different animals, all making different noises, and it was difficult for the china doll to make out much of what was being said. A goose flew past her on its way up to its perch. Sarah called out, "Hello!"

"Honk! What is it? Who's there?" The goose turned around and spotted Sarah. "Honk!" it repeated loudly.

"I'm looking for a treasure chest," Sarah explained. "Perhaps you know of it?"

"Honk! A treasure chest, you say. Yes, I know of it. But what are you willing to pay to have me tell you?"

"Pay you? Oh, dear, I don't have anything much—"

The goose interrupted her. "Is that apron real silk?" it asked.

The china doll looked down at her apron. It was stained with the dirt she had wiped from her face. "Well, yes," she answered. "But it is a little dirty—"

The goose didn't let her finish. "Done!" it said. "I've got the most horrible cold, you see, which is why I keep honking. That apron will keep me warm. Think of it, real silk . . ."

The goose flew Sarah up to the loft where the treasure chest was sitting. How excited the china doll was! This was the end of her search, for certainly the tea set would be inside this great treasure box. The goose helped her unlock the chest and climb in.

The treasure chest was filled with all sorts of things: clothes, shoes that sparkled, a train engine, and an old clock that no longer ticked. In the middle of everything sat a beautiful pale pink tea set. It was made from china, just like Sarah herself, and the moment she saw it, she knew it was perfect. "Jessica will be so happy," she said to herself.

She packed it into an old sock she found in the chest. Then she climbed back over the edge, down to the floor. The goose had waited for her. "Honk! I see you found what you were looking for."

"Yes," said the china doll. "Thank you so much for helping me."

"Oh sure, sure," said the goose. "I'll give you a lift back down if you'd like. Honk!"

"I would like that. Thank you." The china doll climbed onto the back of the goose and held the tea set close to her.

The goose flapped its wings quickly and Sarah lost her grip on the precious package. It fell out of her hands and Sarah tumbled after it—right into a pail of water.

"Honk!" laughed the goose. "You seem to be quite an unlucky doll." Sarah had to agree. Along with her untidy hair, the crack in her forehead, and the dirt and grass stains on her clothing, she was now completely wet.

She reached for the sock that held her tea set, but the rim of the water bucket was too high for her to pull herself out. As she tried to think of a way to escape, a strange rope dangled in front of her.

"Take hold of my tail, doll, and I will pull you out," said a cow.

The china doll gratefully did as the cow suggested, and she and her tea set were soon on dry straw.

"You are most kind," the china doll said. "If there is anything I can do for you, please—"

"Well," answered the cow. "What I want is not so big. I would like a nice red ribbon to tie around my tail."

"Oh," said Sarah. "I do have a red ribbon. Perhaps I might tie it on for you." No sooner said than done. The red ribbon that had once held the key to the treasure chest now made a neat bow around the cow's tail.

"It is but a small thing, but thank you very much," said the cow. "You are indeed a most beautiful doll."

"Thank you," whispered the china doll. It was comforting that the cow had complimented her in spite of her messy clothes and broken face.

The goose waddled up to her. "Honk! I think you need some good luck for a change." The goose pushed some seeds of corn into her hand. "I hope these will help. Honk!"

Sarah thanked the cow and goose and turned to go. She pulled the sock back to the house without running into anyone else. Back at the wall, she searched for the tunnel the rat had led her through. It was so dark the china doll couldn't see very well, but she finally managed to find the entrance. It was even darker inside, and before long she was lost. Before she had time to start worrying, a familiar voice whispered in her ear, "What do you want now?" hissed the rat.

"Please," said the china doll, "please take me back to my room."

"What have you got to give me this time?" the rat asked.

"Give? I haven't anything useful. But perhaps you will take these." The china doll showed the rat the three seeds of corn that the goose had given her.

"Hmm, yes. I will take you to your room in exchange for the corn. Follow me." The rat disappeared quickly into the blackness of the tunnel.

"Wait!" cried the doll. "I cannot see you. I cannot follow you."

The rat came back. "Hold onto my tail," it whispered. "You will be there soon enough."

Obediently Sarah held onto the rat's tail as it pulled her through tunnel after darkened tunnel. When it seemed that they had traveled far longer than before, the rat whispered, "There, up ahead. Do you see it?"

The doll saw nothing. But after a few more steps, she could see a pinprick of light. It was her room! "I will not forget this," Sarah whispered. She waved farewell and breathed in the welcome smell of home. Everything was just as she had left it. The night's adventure had tired Sarah so completely that she didn't even have the energy to climb onto the bed. Instead she sat still where she was.

The door slowly creaked open and Jessica's mother came into the room. When she saw the china doll on the floor, she picked her up and turned her over, examining the wet, dirt-caked clothing and the cracked head. "You must have been through quite an ordeal," said the woman softly. "And what are you doing with the key to my grandmother's chest, hmm?"

The woman spotted the lumpy sock on the floor and peeked inside. Tears came to her eyes when she pulled out the tea set. "This used to be my mother's," she whispered, gently touching a china cup. She remembered tea parties with her mother from her own childhood. She turned back to the doll, murmuring, "I wonder where you . . . how you . . . no matter. Let's see what we can do for you, hmm?"

She carried the china doll downstairs and rummaged in a drawer for her sewing kit. Inside the kit were all sorts of materials: strings, satins, pearls, and little cloth roses. Under the circle of light from the lamp, she set to work making the doll look new again. She fashioned a new bonnet from white lace. She sewed a new dress and apron, white as snow. She polished the doll's shoes and repainted her face. As for the crack in the doll's forehead, she sealed it up with a special glue and painted over it so no one would be able to tell there had ever been a crack at all.

Sarah looked up at the woman. "I am unable to give you anything," she thought. As if reading her thoughts, Jessica's mother whispered, "I don't need anything from you. It is enough that you make my daughter smile." With that she put the final stitch on the china doll's clothing and sat back to survey her work. "Good as new," she said.

She brought Sarah back to her daughter's room and placed her on the pillow where Jessica lay sleeping. She took one last look at the two of them lying together and murmured so softly that the china doll could barely hear, "Thank you."

Sarah turned her black eyes up to Jessica's face, her beloved friend, who was again hugging her so tightly in her sleep. She was excited for the morning, when Jessica would find her gift, but she was very tired from her adventure. Soon Sarah was asleep, dreaming of the many tea parties she and Jessica would share.